Alice Goes to Hollywood

Karen Wallace
ed by Bob Dewar

Black • London

To Susila,
who knows about anteaters – KW

First paperback edition 2006
First published 2005 by
A & C Black Publishers Ltd
37 Soho Square, London, W1D 3QZ

www.acblack.com

ISBN 0-7136-7421-0

A CIP catalogue for this book is available from the British Library.

A&C Black uses paper produced with elemental chlorine-free
pulp, harvested from managed sustained forests.

Printed and bound in Singapore by Tien Wah Press (Pte) Ltd

Chapter One

Alice was an anteater and lived in the jungle.

Every day, she dug for ants with her sharp, curved claws. Then she slurped them up with her long, curling tongue.

When Alice was full, she curled up in a ball and snoozed in the sunshine.

Alice was an anteater. That's what anteaters do.

One day, Alice found a magazine stuck on a thorn bush. It was called *Fabulous Film Stars* and it was all about famous people who made amazing films.

Alice made a big decision. "I'm going to be a film star!" she told the other anteaters. "Just you wait and see."

"Don't be silly, Alice," said the other anteaters. "You're an anteater!"

"Eat up your ants," said her mother, at supper time. "They're your favourite." Alice turned up her snout. "Film stars don't eat ants," she said. "They're tickly, prickly, *yucky* things!"

Days passed. While the other anteaters went to dig up ants, Alice stayed at home and taught herself to tap dance.

While the other anteaters snoozed in the
trees, Alice taught herself to sing.

And when she was alone in the jungle, Alice practised making speeches in different voices.

One afternoon, while the other anteaters were hunting, Alice painted her toenails pink and her lips red. Then she went to see Cornelius the crocodile.

Chapter Two

Cornelius was lying in the water. When he saw Alice, he waddled onto the shore.

Cornelius loved visitors because he loved talking. But sadly Cornelius didn't get many visitors because sometimes he forgot his manners and gobbled them up.

Alice stood far away from Cornelius. She looked at his sharp teeth. "Hello," she said nervously. "How are you?" "Completely full," replied Cornelius. He yawned. His mouth was as big as a cave. "I've heard you want to be a film star." "I *will* be a film star," said Alice.

"I once ate a film star," said Cornelius.
"Would you like to hear about it?"
"No, thank you," said Alice quickly. She
knew that once Cornelius started talking,
it was almost impossible to make him stop.

"How can I help?" asked Cornelius.
"I need clothes to go to Hollywood,"
said Alice.

"Then you must look in my dressing-up
box," replied Cornelius. "It's full of bits
and bobs that I've … uh … collected."

Cornelius ran his tongue along his teeth and waddled back into the water. Alice found the dressing-up box and opened it. She had never seen so many wonderful things…

Alice chose a long blonde wig, a blue
scarf, a pair of high-heeled sandals,
a frilly satin dress, and a pink handbag
shaped like a heart.

She put them on and stared at her
reflection in the water. It was amazing.
She looked just like a film star!
There was just one thing missing…

Alice looked about in the dressing-up
box again and found what she wanted.
A pair of film-star sunglasses!
"Yesss!" she cried, punching the air.

Then, without saying goodbye to anyone, Alice paddled down the river and took the first plane to Hollywood.

Chapter Three

Alice *loved* Hollywood! She loved the
flashing signs, the fast cars and the big,
fancy hotels.

But most of all she loved the film stars.
They crowded around her every day.
"Gee!" they cried. "Aren't you cute?"

Men with huge cameras followed Alice wherever she went. Soon her picture was in all the magazines.

Alice was delighted. "I'm famous!" she cried. "I'm a film star at last!"

She cut out her photograph and sent it
home to the jungle.

There was only one problem…

Alice knew she had to be in a film if she wanted to be a *real* film star. But every time she talked about a job, the film stars asked her the same questions:

"Is it true you live in the jungle?"

"What's it like eating ants?"

One day, Alice met an important film director. He was thin with shiny eyes and looked like a snake.

"I want to be a film star!" said Alice.

"But you're an anteater," said the director.

"An anteater can be a film star!" said Alice.

So Alice showed the director all the things she had taught herself to do. She danced…

She sang…

Doh, Ray, Me, Fa, So, La, Tee, Doh!

She made speeches in different voices...

"Whaddyathink?" asked Alice in her best Hollywood accent.

The director shrugged. "Don't call me, I'll call you," he said.

"What does that mean?" asked Alice.

"It means I don't have any parts for anteaters," said the director.

Chapter Four

That night Alice went to a big, fancy
party. The room was packed with famous
film stars.

Cameras whirred. Flashbulbs popped. All the film stars wanted to have their picture taken with Alice. "Gee!" they cried. "A real live anteater! Is it true you live in the jungle and eat ants?"

Poor Alice! No matter what she said,
they didn't listen. They didn't believe
an anteater could be a film star.

Alice tiptoed outside and sat in the shadows. Two film stars walked onto the balcony.

"Did you hear that anteater?" said one. "Silly animal," said the other. "She thinks she's going to be a film star." They laughed and went back to the party.

Alice crawled under a bush where no one could see her. Tears poured down her wrinkly snout. She thought of all the other anteaters hunting happily in the jungle. And she felt very, very lonely.

"Don't cry, Alice," squeaked a voice.
A hedgehog was standing beside her.
"I saw your picture in the paper,"
he whispered. "I've always wanted to
meet an anteater."

The hedgehog blinked shyly and held out a beautiful gold box. "This is for you." Alice took the box and opened it slowly. It was full of munchy, crunchy ants.

For the first time since she had arrived in Hollywood, Alice felt really hungry.

Alice slurped up the ants with her long, curling tongue. It was as if some kind of spell was broken. Suddenly she knew exactly what she should do!

Chapter Five

Alice pulled off her long blonde wig and ripped her satin dress in two.

She threw away her high-heeled sandals…

… and stamped on her film-star sunglasses.

She was about to throw her handbag away, but she decided not to. Even an anteater needs a handbag sometimes.

"What are you doing?" asked the hedgehog.

"I'm going home," cried Alice happily. "As soon as I tasted those ants I knew I was never meant to be a film star, I'm an anteater, through and through!"

Alice hugged the hedgehog. "Thanks, buddy," she said in a perfect Hollywood accent. "You've done me a big favour." And she planted a kiss on his prickly nose.

The hedgehog trembled all over. It was his dream to be kissed by an anteater. "Come with me," he said in his deepest voice. "I'll take you to the airport."

Chapter Six

The next day, at sunset, Alice arrived on the riverbank. Cornelius was lying in the water. When he saw Alice, he waddled onto the shore. "So how was Hollywood?" he asked. "What were the film stars like?"

Alice pulled a face. "Hollywood was horrible and the film stars were yucky." Cornelius blinked his big yellow eyes. "If you hadn't been in such a hurry, I could have warned you."

"How do *you* know?" asked Alice.

"They don't taste nice," replied Cornelius. He yawned. "It's usually a bad sign."

All the other anteaters were delighted
to see Alice.

Her mother gave her an extra big hug.
"Welcome home!" she cried. "We've
been waiting for you!"

She gave Alice a special supper. There were ants with everything!

Later, when everyone was asleep, Alice watched the moon rise. It shone on the jungle and made it look silver. She turned over and snuggled into her pile of leaves.

For the first time in ages, Alice was completely happy. And she dreamed about ants all night long!